REVF
OF THE
RABBIT

REVENGE OF THE RABBIT

Rose Impey

Illustrated by
André Amstutz

ORCHARD BOOKS

ORCHARD BOOKS
96 Leonard Street, London EC2A 4RH
Orchard Books Australia
14 Mars Road, Lane Cove, NSW 2066
ISBN 1 85213 233 7 (hardback)
ISBN 1 85213 501 8 (paperback)
First published in Great Britain 1990
First paperback publication 1993
Text © Rose Impey 1990
Illustrations © André Amstutz 1990

Printed in Great Britain

CONTENTS

Chapter One

In which we meet the heroines of this story—Pooh and Piglet—and the story begins

At school when everyone else had been picked for a part in the play, or the rounders teams, two people were always left.

"We don't want Pooh," said one team.

"Well, nobody wants Piglet," said the other team. "We'll have to toss for it."

Nobody wanted Pooh because they said she was too big and loud and bossy. But nobody wanted Piglet because she was too small and quiet and wet. Pooh and Piglet couldn't win. They were the sort of girls who don't really fit in.

Neither of them was clever or artistic or good at netball, like Nicola Wicks and her friends. They didn't entertain the class by getting into trouble with Mr Carter and telling rude jokes, like Jason Burke and his gang.

They even looked like the odd ones out.

Pooh, whose real name was Philippa, was the big one. She was tall and, she had to admit it, rather fat. It wasn't that she ate too much; she just ate all the wrong things.

Philippa's mum and dad owned a chip shop called Long John Silver's Fish Bar. Every day, mouthwatering smells of fritters and saveloys and mushy peas drifted up the stairs to their flat. It was exactly the kind of food Philippa enjoyed.

What she didn't enjoy was being called Fatty and Dumpling and Economy-size.

"Oh, take no notice of them," said her mum. "It's not your fault. You can't help the way you're made."

"It's not fair," said Philippa.

"Life never is," said her mum.

Piglet, whose real name was Meena, was the small one, in fact she was tiny. Her mum cooked her appetising curries and bhajees and samosas.

"Eat up, child, or you'll disappear down a crack in the pavement," she told her.

Meena wasn't quite that thin but she had such a small appetite it was no wonder she didn't grow.

"I hate being called Squirt and Tiddler and Weedy," she complained.

"Oh, take no notice of them," said Philippa. "It's not your fault. You can't help the way you're made."

"It's not fair," said Meena.

"Life never is," said Philippa.

People often smiled when they saw the girls together.

"Oh look, here come Winnie the Pooh and Piglet," said Nicola Wicks one day. And because Nicola Wicks was the boss of Class 4 everyone laughed and the nicknames seemed to stick.

9

The girls didn't mind; they quite liked the names. They made them feel like a special pair—Batman and Robin, Cagney and Lacey, Pooh and Piglet—a dynamic duo, always ready to do good deeds and defend the underdog.

Or in this particular story...the under-rabbit.

And here is where our story really begins:

It was almost three o'clock, the rest of Class 4 was out at Games, but Pooh and Piglet had been excused, so that they could search for Pooh's PE kit. They hadn't found it, of course, because it was in the washing basket at home. They hadn't told Mr Carter that or he would have made them do Games in their ordinary clothes and Pooh and Piglet didn't like Games. They preferred poking around the cloakrooms. It was surprising what they discovered by keeping their heads down and staying quiet. Today was a good example.

Coming along the corridor grumbling to himself was Mr Benson, the school caretaker. (He's one of the baddies in this story.) In the other direction came Mrs Riley, the headteacher. (She isn't.) The two girls bobbed down behind the coatracks and listened.

"There you are," said the caretaker. "I've been looking for you."

Mrs Riley's heart sank. She usually tried to avoid the caretaker when he was in a bad mood. Mr Benson waved his right hand under Mrs Riley's nose. It was wrapped in a clean yellow duster.

"This is the final straw, Mrs Riley. Either that rabbit goes, or I go."

"Oh, Mr Benson, not again." Snuggles, the school rabbit, had obviously bitten him. It wasn't the first time. "I am sorry," said Mrs Riley.

"You being sorry won't help me when I'm dying of rabies."

Mrs Riley smiled. "I shouldn't think Snuggles has rabies."

"Well, we'll soon find out, won't we," he snapped.

The head sighed.

"That rabbit wants dealing with—great bad-tempered beast—always snapping and hissing at people," hissed the caretaker. "It's not right, keeping it locked up in a hutch all day. It smells terrible."

"Yes, I know," she said. The rabbit was a problem. "But what can we do about it?"

"You leave it to me. I'll *deal* with it." There was an evil look in the caretaker's eye. "I'll put it out of its misery."

"Mr Benson!" Mrs Riley was shocked.

So were Pooh and Piglet. It was all Pooh could do to keep quiet at this point. She was tempted to rush out and bite the caretaker herself.

As if she sensed their presence, the head glanced around anxiously and lowered her voice. "Whatever would I tell the infants?"

"You could tell them it died—of a bad temper."

Mrs Riley was not amused.

"You could tell them it escaped."

Right now Mrs Riley wished it would.

"You could tell them when I opened up in the morning there it was . . . gone."

"Perhaps *you'd* like to tell them," she said, "since it's your idea. I can assure you, they'd be very upset."

"Upset! You mean relieved. The whole school's scared of it. But I'm the one it bites. Well, not any more."

"I shall have to think very carefully about this," she said. "I don't want a death on my conscience."

"It's only a rabbit, Mrs Riley."

Mrs Riley decided to ignore this remark. "I'm very busy, you'll have to excuse me," she said. "I'll let you know what I decide."

She walked away, leaving the caretaker in the junior cloakroom. He opened the duster and inspected his bloodstained hand.

"Wretched animal," he muttered, "your days are numbered." Then he went to the secretary's office in search of the first aid kit.

Two faces—one small and brown, one large and very pink—appeared over the coathooks, checking the coast was clear. Pooh and Piglet breathed heavily and crept out from behind the anoraks and PE bags.

"Honestly," said Pooh. "Did you hear that?"

"Poor Snuggles," said Piglet.

"It shouldn't be allowed. Someone should put a stop to it." Pooh began to smile. "*Someone* should set that rabbit free."

Piglet nodded. She knew who Pooh meant. Putting things right was their main hobby. The two girls were continually on the lookout for some helpless creature to protect.

However, Piglet wasn't sure that Snuggles came into the category of "helpless creature". He was so big and rather fierce. She hesitated for a moment but Pooh was already decided.

"Come on," she said. And the girls raced off to visit the condemned rabbit.

Now we shall meet Snuggles—the innocent victim of this story—well, the victim anyway.

Snuggles' hutch was at the end of a corridor which led to the kiln-room. The kiln had been broken since last term so it had seemed to the caretaker an ideal place to keep the school pet—well away from any children.

The girls stared at Snuggles and Snuggles stared back.

"Poor dumb animal," said Pooh. "How would Mr Benson like it if someone decided to put him out of his misery, just because he's bad-tempered?"

Piglet giggled. Mr Benson's days would certainly be numbered, she thought. The caretaker suffered from back trouble, which made him very irritable; he was always telling people off.

Pooh felt a swell of sympathy for the rabbit. Nobody liked you if you were too big. She knew this from bitter experience.

"Do you remember when we were in the infants, Snuggles was so sweet and cuddly then?"

Piglet sighed. "He's grown," she said.

"Of course he's grown. Even you've grown a bit since then. He can't help it. It doesn't mean he's not still soft and sweet inside."

Pooh put her hand to the wire mesh to stroke the rabbit's sweet black nose.
But Snuggles drew back his upper lip and made a strange choking sound in his throat.
The girls quickly moved away.

Piglet put her hand over her nose. "Ooh, he smells."

"So would you if no one ever cleaned you out. It's disgusting."

The girls both felt guilty. Piglet sighed.

"Well, now it's up to us," said Pooh. "Are we going to let this poor defenceless animal be murdered in cold blood?"

"No," said Piglet.

"This innocent creature that never did anyone any harm..."

"He bit the caretaker," Piglet reminded Pooh.

"I don't blame him," said Pooh. "Locked up in this horrible hutch, no wonder he's a bit bad-tempered." It made her bad-tempered just thinking about it.

Checking to see that no one was coming, Pooh pulled the sleeve of her sweater down to protect her hand and reached out to open the hutch door.

17

The rabbit rose up on his back legs, ready to spring forward. He was awfully big—the size of a small dog. He bared his teeth and hissed again. Pooh lost her nerve and drew back. Piglet edged behind her and peeped out.

"Oh, Pooh," she said, "look at his teeth."

As if to save them, the bell suddenly rang. There was mass scraping of chairs as nearby classes got ready to go home.

"Come on," said Pooh. "We'll come back tomorrow."

"But Pooh—"

18

As usual Pooh didn't stop to hear. She was already heading off along the corridor. Piglet often had to run to keep up with her, especially when it was home time. If Pooh *had* bothered to stop she would have discovered sooner what Piglet was trying to tell her—that tomorrow was Saturday.

Chapter Two

In which we meet the other baddies in this story—the netball team—and the rabbit gets his freedom

Pooh and Piglet stepped out onto the playground. Their path was blocked by a group of girls from Class 4, led as usual by Nicola Wicks—boss of the class and captain of the netball team.

"Well, look who's here. Poohey and Piggy, Wimps of the Year."

"Where have you two been all lesson?" asked Andrea Armstrong.

"Mind your own business," said Pooh.

"They've been skiving, of course," said Melanie Powell.

"Poking around the cloakroom, I'll bet," said Nicola.

Pooh and Piglet blushed; they could hardly deny it.

"I don't see why they should get out of Games, everyone else has to do it," said Surendra Patel.

"Neither do I," agreed Nicola, stepping forward. The netballers closed in behind her.

"Just get lost, will you," said Pooh, "or else..."

"Or else what?" said Nicola, poking Pooh painfully in the chest.

Given her size, Pooh felt more than a match for any of the girls individually, but she wasn't so sure about all of them together. Piglet of course didn't feel a match for anyone.

"Come on," she said, tugging at Pooh's sleeve. "I've got to get home."

Pooh ducked quickly between the girls.

"Out of the way," she said.

She walked determinedly towards the gate and Piglet followed. When they were a safe distance away Pooh called back over her shoulder, "If that's what exercise does for you, I'm glad I'm a wimp."

Piglet kept her head down and the girls hurried on home.

"I don't know why they're always picking on us," Piglet complained.

"Never mind about them," said Pooh. "We've got more important things to think about. You come to my house tonight and we'll make a plan of action. Then tomorrow..." she lowered her voice, "...we'll set Snuggles free."

"Pooh..." Piglet began again.

"We'll wear masks, like those Animal Rights people," said Pooh, getting very excited. "Then no one'll recognise us."

"But Pooh, tomorrow's Saturday," Piglet finally managed to say.

Pooh stopped dead in the middle of the pavement and two little infants walked straight into her, as if a tree had unexpectedly sprung up in their path.

"Why didn't you say that before?"

Piglet shrugged. "I tried."

"Well, we'll just have to go back, won't we?"

"What, now?"

"It may be too late by Monday," said Pooh.

Piglet nodded. She couldn't bear to think about that.

The girls retraced their steps, ignoring the curious stares they got heading in the wrong direction. They sneaked into the school building and checked each of the classrooms to find out where the cleaners were. Then they tiptoed along the corridor. The school felt completely  empty and every sound they made echoed around the walls. The girls hardly dared to breathe. When they reached his hutch they found Snuggles curled up, with his back to them, sound asleep.

"He's asleep," whispered Piglet.

"I can see that," whispered Pooh. "He'll soon wake up. I'll open the cage. You go and open the door so he can make a quick getaway."

Piglet went to the fire door at the end of the corridor which opened directly onto the school field. She had to swing her full weight against it before she managed to open it. It made a terrible clatter. Then she stood right back against the kiln-room door, leaving plenty of space for the rabbit to pass her.

Pooh carefully undid the catch. "Wakey, wakey," she whispered. "Freedom at last."

They both stood well back and waited, but the rabbit slept on.

"Time to go, you dozy thing," said Pooh, lightly prodding the rabbit's bottom. Snuggles stirred, moved his weight into a different position, then slept on soundly.

Piglet was beginning to get nervous. Any moment she expected the caretaker or Mrs Riley to appear and catch them red-handed.

"Perhaps he doesn't want to escape," she whispered. "Perhaps he likes it here. Perhaps we should leave him."

Pooh gave her a withering look. "Would you like it here? Talk some sense, girl. This rabbit wants his freedom . . . he just doesn't realise it *yet*!" And she gave the rabbit a much harder prod.

This time Snuggles woke and sat up. He scratched himself behind the ear with his back paw, then turned round. Slowly he seemed to notice that something was different. Uncertainly he took a step outside onto the worktop.

The large animal peered down at the floor, as if estimating his chances of reaching it in one piece.

"Go on," said Pooh. "You can do it." She waved her arms in an encouraging way but stopped short of actually giving Snuggles a lift down.

The rabbit looked like a swimmer who suspects the water is cold but at last decides to brave it. He jumped and landed on the corridor floor with a loud THUD, giving the girls some idea of his enormous weight.

Then, unfortunately, instead of hopping off down the corridor as they'd intended, Snuggles discovered a huge opened bag of rabbit food.

"Oh no," groaned Pooh.

"Oh, Pooh, stop him," moaned Piglet. She had visions of the rabbit eating his way through a whole month's supply of food and expanding like a balloon until he filled the corridor and couldn't fit through the door. It reminded Piglet of a horror film she'd once seen.

"What do you mean *stop him*," hissed Pooh. "What do you suggest?"

Piglet had no suggestions. So Pooh got

behind the rabbit and tried to encourage him towards the door.

"Come on this way, nice little rabbit," she said.

Suddenly the girls heard heavy footsteps coming along the corridor from the direction of the infant's cloakroom. It had to be the caretaker.

"Come on, quick," said Piglet, gesturing wildly at Pooh. She was already halfway through the door herself. But Pooh was determined to have one more try. She put her hands under his bottom and attempted to launch the rabbit forward like a missile.

Snuggles turned round and once more showed her his huge teeth. Pooh backed off.

"We'll just have to leave you then, you stubborn animal," she said. And the girls headed off through the fire door and across the school field.

They kept on running until they reached the cover of a small wood which marked the school boundary. As soon as it was safe they stopped to get their breath. They turned and looked back. Piglet squealed.

The girls were horrified to see a large furry figure hopping at some speed across the field, heading in their direction.

"Oh no, he's following us," said Pooh.

"What are we going to do?" said Piglet.

"We're going home," said Pooh. "Come on. Quick."

Chapter Three

In which Mr Benson gets his come-uppance—well, the first part of it—and Mrs Riley jumps to conclusions

The heavy footsteps echoed down the silent corridor. It *was* Mr Benson, carrying a large sweeping brush and a black plastic sack. He was still in a bad mood. The moment he turned the corner he saw the fire door standing wide open. He was about to close it when he noticed another door, also wide open, revealing a completely empty rabbit hutch. He dropped the brush with a clatter.

"Oh, flipping heck," he muttered. "I don't believe this."

The caretaker knew straight away who'd done it. It was typical of Mrs Riley. She was like his wife, really soft when it came to animals. She was pretty soft with the kids too, in his opinion. It was a mystery to Mr Benson how she had ever managed to run this school, before he came.

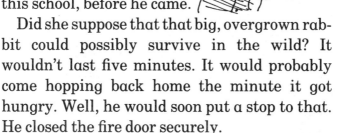

Flipping heck!

Did she suppose that that big, overgrown rabbit could possibly survive in the wild? It wouldn't last five minutes. It would probably come hopping back home the minute it got hungry. Well, he would soon put a stop to that. He closed the fire door securely.

"That'll keep it out," he muttered, "smelly object."

And while he was about it, he thought, he

would get rid of its hutch, before one of the teachers spotted it and decided to fill it with another animal, that *he'd* be left to look after.

The caretaker closed the door and tilted the hutch forward. He slid his fingers underneath. He eased it towards him, bending his body slightly to take the strain. Then he heaved.

"Gordon Bennett!" he yelled.

There was a familiar, sickening click in his spine. His back had gone. He stood there completely locked for a moment, unable to move in any direction.

Slowly he allowed the hutch to fall back onto the worktop. The entire weight of it landed on his fingers. This time Mr Benson really swore and he didn't care who heard him.

Almost in tears, he eased out one hand and then the other. Each small movement made him gasp. Bent forward with the pain and leaning considerably sideways, the caretaker tottered away down the corridor. He looked like the crooked man in the nursery rhyme.

It was that wretched animal he had to thank for this. Oh, it was a good job the rabbit had escaped. If Mr Benson had got hold of it just then he'd have turned it into a small fur coat. Mr Benson was *not* an animal lover, not by any stretch of the imagination.

But Mrs Riley was.

She had two cats

and a goldfish at home

and she'd had a dog for years until it finally died of old age. The headteacher was sitting in her office, thinking of all the assemblies she had done over the years on caring for animals, protecting endangered species, supporting The World Wildlife Fund.

34

So she felt very guilty about the school rabbit. She knew Snuggles had been neglected. It was hardly his fault that he wasn't a fluffy, sweet-tempered bunny any more. That was no reason to kill the rabbit off.

But on the other hand, they had to do something about him. He was far too big for the school. She wondered if they could advertise for a new owner, some rabbit lover who'd give him a good home. Why hadn't she thought of that before? It was so obvious. She would go and tell the caretaker right now. She had learnt from experience that you had to keep Mr Benson firmly in his place.

She looked for him in the hall and then searched the rest of the school, but he wasn't there. No one had seen him for the past half hour. Well, it would have to wait until tomorrow. Mrs Riley had an appointment with her dentist which she'd been dreading for days. On her way out she thought she would look in on Snuggles, to ease her guilty conscience.

When she discovered the empty cage and the missing rabbit, combined with the missing caretaker, Mrs Riley jumped to the obvious conclusion.

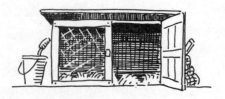

Mr Benson had done the dirty deed, already, without waiting for her decision. Oh, this time the caretaker had gone too far.

Just then, to add to the confusion, the netball team, having finished their practice, appeared on the scene. They were hoping to persuade Mrs Riley to buy them a new set of netball bibs. They were fed up with the present ones. Mud-brown and purple weren't very attractive colours, in their opinion.

"Oh, there you are, Mrs Riley. We've been

looking for you," Nicola began, but she was interrupted by cries from the others.

"Oh, look!"

"Ahhhh!" said Andrea.

"Where's Snuggles?" demanded Melanie.

For a moment Mrs Riley struggled with her conscience and then decided to lie—or at least conceal the truth.

"Ermmm, I don't know," she replied. "I just got here, and there he was . . . gone."

"Somebody must have let him out," said Nicola accusingly.

"Oh, yes," agreed the head. "*Somebody* must have."

"What are you going to do?" asked Andrea.

Mrs Riley hesitated.

"You could offer a reward," suggested Nicola.

"A reward?" The head looked doubtful but the girls quickly warmed to the idea.

"Out of School Fund."

"Five pounds for whoever finds Snuggles first."

"Me."

"It'll be me."

"I will." They all shouted at once.

"We'll get the whole team out searching," Nicola offered.

Mrs Riley was horrified. "Oh, I wouldn't do

that. I'm afraid it's too late." The girls looked at her in surprise. "I mean...where would you start? He could be...anywhere."

"First we'll search the school," said Nicola.

"Then we'll search the grounds," said Andrea.

"Then we'll search the whole town," said Surendra.

"We'll put posters up."

"Advertise on local radio."

"My dad'll put it in the papers."

The girls got completely carried away.

"Oh, no, don't do that," begged Mrs Riley, "not yet. He might turn up, you know. Perhaps we should wait until tomorrow and see. I think that's the best idea. I have to go. I've got a dentist's appointment and I'm late already."

"Don't you worry about it. You go, miss. We'll take care of it. We'll start now," said Nicola, issuing instructions. "You go that way. You take the infant hall and cloakrooms. You do the art area . . ." Girls raced off in all directions. She glanced back and for the first time noticed how upset the headteacher seemed.

"Ahh, don't you worry, Mrs Riley." She patted her arm. "If Snuggles is still here we'll find him and if he's not . . . we'll report his disappearance to the police." And Nicola went off too.

Mrs Riley's heart sank. "Oh, no," she groaned. That wretched caretaker! Look what he'd started. It was a good job he'd disappeared. If she had found him just then, Mr Benson would have wished he had never got out of bed that morning.

In fact, at that moment, it's exactly what Mr Benson *was* wishing. It definitely hadn't been his day—he'd been bitten by a rabbit and now he'd put his back out.

The caretaker lay flat on the boiler-room floor. He knew from experience that lying on a hard, flat surface was the only thing which relieved back pain. He closed his eyes and practised deep breathing. He tried to relax. He promised himself he wouldn't think about that rabbit. He would pretend it had never existed. Mr Benson breathed slowly and deeply and soon he was fast asleep.

Chapter Four

In which we return to our heroines—who are also beginning to wish they hadn't got out of bed that morning

Without a backward glance at the huge rabbit bounding towards them, the girls set off for home at a run.

"He's free now," said Pooh. "He doesn't need us." She felt sure that Snuggles was perfectly able to look after himself.

The girls raced through the trees for a few metres then, by means of a broken fence, got out onto a path. This led to a small industrial estate and eventually to the row of shops down from the fish bar where Pooh lived.

Quite soon the girls tired and started to walk, Pooh with an innocent air but Piglet peering guiltily over her shoulder.

"Oh, Pooh, he's still behind us," she wailed.

"Don't worry. He's bound to get tired and give

up," Pooh told her. But both girls started to run again just in case.

It occurred to Pooh that it was typical of their luck, that having gone to so much trouble to get out of Games they should find themselves taking all this unwanted exercise.

If only the rabbit had had the sense to stay around the school grounds. That was a perfectly suitable place for a rabbit, she thought. This wasn't, concrete and glass everywhere. A rabbit the size of a dog would quickly draw attention to itself, wandering around an industrial estate.

The girls ran until their lungs were bursting. But Snuggles was clearly determined to keep up with them. Since there seemed no chance of losing him, Pooh abruptly stopped and turned to face the rabbit. She tried to look brave.

"It's important not to show your fear," she told Piglet. "Animals can smell it, you know." Pooh had read this once in a book about lion-tamers.

Piglet tried in vain not to show *her* fear but it was written all over her face. The rabbit could have spotted her fear a mile away. He moved towards her, as if to get a closer look.

"Back...back," said Pooh, sternly pointing her finger. "Sit!" To her complete surprise the rabbit sat back on his haunches. Piglet gazed up at Pooh in admiration. Pooh smiled.

"Sta-a-ay," she said.

Snuggles sat up straight, like a well-trained dog, and stayed.

Pooh knew her good luck couldn't last. In a couple of minutes they'd be home. They must shake the rabbit off somehow.

"We need to keep him busy," she whispered. "Then we can give him the slip."

As though he'd heard and understood, the rabbit immediately edged forward.

"Stay! Good rabbit. Stay!" Pooh growled at

him. She fixed him with her eye. "Si-i-it."

Again Snuggles sank back and waited. His black nose twitched. He seemed to be considering his next move.

Piglet waited too. She would have preferred to run as fast as her little legs would carry her, away from this terrifying rabbit, which was rapidly turning into a monster in her imagination. She could see that she would never outrun him. Standing still, however, was almost more than she could bear.

Piglet couldn't begin to understand Pooh's next comment.

"If only I hadn't eaten all my sandwiches."

How could Pooh possibly feel hungry at a time like this, Piglet wondered?

"Have *you* got any left?" asked Pooh, her eyes fixed on the rabbit's. Piglet nodded. She always had lunch left, surely Pooh knew that.

"Well, hand it over," Pooh whispered.

Very slowly, avoiding any sudden moves, she undid her schoolbag, took out her box and gave Pooh the sandwiches. They looked tired and soggy; Pooh was welcome to them.

"What sort are they?"

"Lettuce and tomato."

"Perfect," breathed Pooh. She broke the sandwiches into small pieces and laid a trail

across the path and through the fence into the
back yard of the laundry.

"Sit," she warned the rabbit, each time it
twitched.

When Pooh stepped back out of the way
Snuggles sniffed the first piece, gobbled it up,
sniffed his way to the next and ate that too. The
chase had clearly given him an appetite.

"That's it, he's hooked. Now's our chance.
Let's go."

The girls moved quickly, but quietly, to avoid
disturbing the rabbit. They turned a corner and
looking back had their final glimpse of Snuggles nibbling his way through two lettuce and
tomato sandwiches. Free at last, they headed
off home as fast as they could.

Meanwhile, back at school, the unhappy caretaker was waiting to lock up. It was getting on
for five o'clock. Mr Benson had woken feeling

stiff and sore and completely confused in the dark boiler-room. It had seemed like hours before he remembered what he was doing there and even longer before he was able to roll over and lift himself off the floor. All he wanted now was to stagger home to his bungalow and lie flat on his back on the sitting room carpet.

Unfortunately he was prevented from doing this because the netball girls had left their clothes strewn around the cloakroom. He had no idea what they were doing. He could see them in their shorts, racing about the school field, running into the bushes and then out again. It looked like circuit training but there was no sign of a teacher with them.

He opened the window and yelled to them, "Get off home, can't you? I want to lock up."

They rushed back in, spreading mud and grass cuttings over his clean floors.

Get off home!

"Out!" ordered Mr Benson.

The girls trooped out and then tiptoed back in, barefoot this time, leaving sweaty footprints instead.

"What are you doing, still here at this time?" he demanded.

"We've been searching for Snuggles," said Nicola.

"Someone let him out," said Andrea.

"Really," said the caretaker.

"Mrs Riley found his empty cage."

"We were there," said Surendra.

"There's a reward," Melanie told him.

"Five pounds," said Nicola.

"Five pounds!" said the caretaker, incredulous.

"Out of School Fund," said Andrea.

"I don't believe this."

"It's true," Melanie insisted.

"So did you find him?"

"No." The girls were very disappointed.

The caretaker wasn't. "Oh, what a shame," he said. "Never mind. Time you were going home. Come on. I want to lock up."

As the netball girls walked home they observed, not for the first time, that the caretaker was a miserable old devil.

"He didn't look a bit bothered about Snuggles, did he?" said Nicola.

"He's a heartless brute," said Melanie, "just like my dad." Melanie's father had survived two years of her campaign to get a dog and he wasn't showing any signs of weakening.

"Who cares about Mr Benson?" said Surendra. "We're not going to let him put us off, are we?"

"Not on your life," said Nicola. "There's five pounds reward."

"If one of us finds him I think we should share the money," said Andrea. Nicola wasn't sure. Should any of the others find him she approved of the idea, but if she found him...that was different.

"All right," she said, her fingers crossed tightly behind her back. The other two also nodded.

However when the girls split up and went on home, they were each busy planning in detail how *they* would spend the five pounds, if they found Snuggles first.

So you can see they were not what you'd call *good* friends, unlike our heroines. Pooh and Piglet always stick together, come what may, which is a good job because from now on ... *things get worse and worse.*

Chapter Five

In which things start to get worse and Pooh and Piglet hide in a shed

Leaving Snuggles far behind Pooh and Piglet passed the newer shops with their shared car park, then reached the older ones, which had their own individual back gardens. They opened Pooh's gate, slipped through and fastened it behind them.

The girls didn't breathe easily until they were inside the building. They raced up the back stairs into Pooh's flat. Her mum and dad were already downstairs, getting ready for five o'clock, which was opening time.

They threw themselves onto the sofa, their hearts still pounding. At last Pooh began to grin. She let out a loud cheer.

"Yippee, we did it. We saved that poor rabbit's life."

Piglet smiled too, thankful it was all over. Then she noticed the time. She jumped up.

"I'm late. I've got to go. I've got dancing practice at five."

"Again?" said Pooh.

Piglet was practising for Diwali. She'd been practising for weeks.

"It's a very difficult dance," she said.

"I'll see you tomorrow," said Pooh. And Piglet left.

Pooh sat for a few moments before she noticed her stomach was terribly empty. She got up to look for her mum, to see what was for tea. But instead she found Piglet on the stairs.

"You're soon back."

"He's down there," said Piglet. "He's waiting in the lane."

Pooh heard a loud noise, a steady, dull thumping sound coming from the garden.

"Whatever's that?" she asked.

"It's him," said Piglet. "He's trying to get in."

51

"Philippa, is that you up there?" called Pooh's mum. "Go and see who's banging on our gate, will you? Your dad and I are busy down here."

"I was just going," called Pooh.

"Well, hurry up. Whoever it is'll have the gate down in a minute. Some people have got no patience."

Pooh and Piglet raced down the stairs. The banging was getting louder all the time.

"What are you going to do?" asked Piglet.

"I'll have to let him in, won't I?"

"Oh, don't," she begged.

"What else can we do?"

Piglet shrugged.

"Exactly," said Pooh. She opened the gate and in bounded Snuggles.

The rabbit, one hop at a time, advanced on them, forcing the girls into a corner. He drew back his upper lip and began hissing at them.

"D-d-don't let him see your f-f-fear," Piglet reminded Pooh.

But Pooh wasn't feeling very brave any more.
"Quick, in here." She dragged Piglet towards
the garden shed and they both ducked inside,
pulling the door closed behind them. Piglet
gave a heavy sigh and dropped her schoolbag on
the floor. They each sank down onto a crate of
pop bottles and sat staring at one another.

"Why's he so angry with us?" asked Piglet. "We're the ones who saved his life."

"You can't expect him to understand that. Rabbit's aren't the most intelligent animals in the world. They've only got small brains."

As if he'd heard the remark, and taken exception to it, the rabbit began to scratch viciously at the door. Both girls shot up. Pooh tried to peer out of the window but it was too high up and only offered a view of the washing line.

"What do you think he'd do, if he got in here?" asked Piglet.

"He would probably bite us," said Pooh, "the mood he's in."

"Would he eat us?"

"No, of course he wouldn't eat us. Rabbits are vegetarians."

"All of them?"

"All of them," said Pooh.

Piglet began to relax. The girls sat down again.

"I'm going to be in real trouble, you know," said Piglet.

"Well, I can't help that."

"Well, we can't stay here for ever," said Piglet.

"This is the wrong way round, you know," said Pooh. "It's Snuggles should be in here and us outside."

"If we could persuade him in," said Piglet, "we could slip out." Judging by the noise he was making, Snuggles wouldn't take much persuasion.

"It's worth a try," said Pooh. "But I think we ought to arm ourselves, just in case." Piglet began to feel anxious again.

The girls looked around for likely weapons. There was an assortment of garden tools:

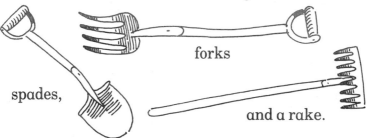

forks

spades,

and a rake.

Pooh took a spade;
Piglet took the rake
and a leather gardening
glove. They squeezed together
behind the door
and carefully pulled it open a crack.

"Ready?" whispered Pooh.

Piglet nodded. They waited, almost shaking with anticipation, expecting the rabbit to rush in, but nothing happened. So Pooh put her nose around the door to see where he'd gone.

Suddenly she let out a shriek. "Oh, you monster. My mum'll shoot you."

She rushed towards the rabbit who was completely submerged in a huge hole he had dug in the shrubbery. His paws were working like a mechanical digger. Soil was flying in all directions, showering the girls. Two rose bushes lay on their sides. The hole was already large

56

enough to bury a small body. And for a moment Pooh had a good idea whose body it ought to be.

"Stop that, you rotten rodent," she shouted. She couldn't immediately think of a more insulting name for the animal. "Stop it! Do you hear me?"

Snuggles again seemed to recognise the authority in Pooh's voice and did as he was told. He sat quietly in the hole, watching them.

"Get out of that hole. Right now."

The rabbit climbed out and came towards them. In terror Piglet threw him the gardening glove she had armed herself with. The rabbit sniffed it, then picked it up in his teeth. He approached the girls, carrying the glove like a cat bearing a dead mouse.

The girls, armed with their weapons, advanced on Snuggles as if they were a pair of lion-tamers.

They guided him towards the open shed. The moment he was inside they threw their full weight against the door and locked it. They leaned on it, panting.

"This rabbit's turning out to be more trouble than enough," said Pooh. "We've got to get rid of him."

"Couldn't we leave him there till tomorrow?" said Piglet.

"What if he starts banging again? It's okay for you. You can go home and do your Diwali dancing. I'm the one left babysitting Rambo."

Piglet giggled. The name suited the rabbit much better. He might have looked like a Snuggles once upon a time, but he was definitely more of a Rambo now.

Pooh climbed onto a pile of bricks stacked against the shed and peeped in through the window. She could just make out a white shape slowly exploring from side to side.

"He seems quiet for the moment. You'd better get off home. I'll see you in the morning." But Piglet stood there, hovering. "Now what are you waiting for?"

"My bag."

Pooh didn't need to ask where she'd left it. "Oh, honestly," she said. "You'll have to manage without it, unless you'd rather go in and get it?"

But Piglet shook her head. Wild horses wouldn't have dragged her back into that shed.

"Philippa, it's time you had your tea," her mum called.

"Coming, Mum," Pooh called back. "I'm starving."

Inside the shed Snuggles sniffed each corner,

looking for a suitable place to curl up. The softest thing he could find for a bed was Piglet's schoolbag. Snuggles dragged it by his teeth into a convenient spot, curled up on top of it and fell asleep.

In his dream a large, sullen face pressed itself against the door of his hutch. It was the face of the enemy. Even without seeing him, Snuggles would know him by his smell: disinfectant and floor polish mixed with the stale smell of the caretaker's pipe tobacco.

Rough, red hands reached into his hutch. The hands of the enemy seized hold of him and dangled him in mid-air until the rabbit felt dizzy and terrified. In his terror Snuggles sank his teeth into that rough, red hand. The enemy let out a terrible cry and fled.

Snuggles dreamed on. In his dream he imagined how one day he would get his revenge on the enemy.

Chapter Six

*In which Pooh learns some unpleasant facts,
and wishes she hadn't*

After tea Pooh crept out to check up on Snuggles. As far as she could make out, he was still sleeping. He was probably dreaming about lettuce and tomato sandwiches, she thought, leading off in a never-ending trail.

How were they going to get rid of him, she wondered? Perhaps before she went to bed, she could slip out in the dark. She could open the shed door and the back gate, and by the morning hopefully he would have disappeared.

Of course, as you will know, things rarely work out so simply, nor do they on this occasion.

"Philippa, are you coming?" her mum called. Pooh went in to the fish bar to do her Friday night jobs. She wasn't very keen on this. She was always afraid of being seen there by anyone from school. However, if she didn't do them she didn't get her pocket money.

She arranged the shelves with bottles of pop and jars of pickled onions, refilled the salt and vinegar containers on the bar and organised extra piles of paper.

In a quiet moment, when the shop was almost empty, Pooh's mum asked, "Who *was* that banging on our gate earlier?"

"No one," said Pooh.

"What do you mean, no one?"

"Just some kids fooling round." Her mum looked up suspiciously. "Oh, it was no one," said Pooh. "No one you'd know." Fortunately her dad suddenly changed the subject.

"Have you heard about that school rabbit disappearing, Philippa?"

Pooh dropped the pile of paper she was stacking all over the floor. Her face turned the colour of the bottled beetroot she'd been arranging on the shelf.

"Oh, Philippa, pick them up quickly. It's just as well we keep this floor so clean. What rabbit's that?" her mum asked her dad.

"Some pet rabbit they've got at school."

"Snuggles," said Pooh, keeping her head down.

"I remember him. You once brought him home when you were in the infants," said her mum. "He was a sweet little thing."

"Well, it seems some idiot has left his cage door open and the poor thing's escaped."

"Did you know about it, Philippa?" her mum asked.

Pooh couldn't trust herself to speak again. She shook her head.

£5
REWARD
Have you seen
SNUGGLES?

"That Wicks girl was in earlier," said her dad, "the one out of your class. She asked me to put up a *missing rabbit* poster. I told her if we found him we could put him on the menu:

Tonight's Special—Fried Rabbit and Chips."

"Dad!"

"Oh, Bernard. Fancy saying that."

Pooh's dad laughed. "She didn't seem very amused either. She said, 'That's not funny, Mr Curtis. There's a five pound reward you know, for anyone who finds him.'"

"A reward!" said Pooh. This was news to her.

"Poor creature," said Pooh's mum. "I hate to think of animals caged up, it's cruel. I'm glad he's escaped. I'd have let him out if I'd been there."

Pooh looked at her mum in admiration. She was tempted to own up and say, "We did it, Mum. Me and Piglet let him out." But her dad's words stopped her in time.

"Don't be daft. You can't let domestic pets out into the wild like that; they'd never survive; they're too soft. That rabbit'll probably starve to death, unless some other animal gets him first."

Pooh couldn't keep quiet. "Oh, Dad, he'd be able to look after himself. You should see him. He's enormous."

"So were the dinosaurs, but they died out. He won't be fast enough on his feet."

"You should see him run. You should see his teeth."

"Oh, take no notice of your dad. He likes to look on the bad side," said Pooh's mum. "There's plenty of grass for him to eat. He'll dig himself a burrow."

"He won't know how," said her dad. "I'll bet he's never dug a proper hole in his life."

"He has," said Pooh. "You should see the one in our shrubbery."

"*Our* shrubbery?" said her mum.

"At school," said Pooh, thinking on her feet.

"The school shrubbery."

"Even so, pet rabbits are not meant to run wild," said her dad.

"How come you're such an authority on rabbits?" asked her mum.

"Harold breeds 'em. He's got dozens of different sorts, real champions. The rare ones are worth a packet, Harold says."

Harold and Pooh's dad were in the same St John's Ambulance team. They went off together sometimes on a Saturday, in their black and white uniforms. It sounded dead boring to Pooh, standing there for hours in case someone should faint at a garden fête, or have a heart attack. Pooh had often wondered what her dad and Harold found to do all day. Obviously they talked about rabbits.

"Mark my words," said her dad. "He won't even last the night."

Pooh's eyes filled up.

"Oh, Philippa, you are a softy. You're not going to start crying, are you?" asked her mum. "You'd think it was your rabbit to look at your face."

Pooh said, "I'm going out."

"Where are you going?"

"To call for Piglet."

"I do wish you wouldn't call her that daft name. Her name's Meena." Pooh ignored her mum. "Well, don't be late. And don't get up to mischief."

"And leave the lads alone," said her dad.

Pooh glared at him and walked out.

"You do tease her," said her mum. "Fancy telling her all about that rabbit. She'll be worried now, she's so sensitive."

"She's just like you," said Pooh's dad, "soft as a brush."

"Soft, am I?" said Pooh's mum. She aimed the wet cloth she was using to clean the bar straight at him. Pooh's dad turned round and caught it full in the face. That made the customers laugh.

Pooh half ran to Piglet's house. She was bursting to tell her the bad news. Whatever were they going to do with Snuggles? If only they could get the rabbit back into school without anybody seeing them. But how? That was the question.

Chapter Seven

In which Piglet has a bright idea and Pooh cheers up

Pooh knocked on Meena's door. Her father answered.

"Why, come in, Philippa," he said in his careful, charming way. "I'll tell Meena you are here. She'll be pleased to see you."

Meena's father was a doctor. He always talked like this to Pooh, as if she was visiting royalty, or as if she and Piglet hadn't seen each other for weeks. It embarrassed her. She hung back in the porch.

"Meena, your friend Philippa is here," her father called.

Meena's two little sisters peeped round the door, grinning.

"Hi," said Pooh. The little girls magically disappeared.

Piglet came downstairs wearing a bright yellow sari. She smiled at Pooh; they both blushed.

"Aren't you going to invite your friend in?" her father asked.

Piglet looked sideways at Pooh, who half shook her head.

"Can we go upstairs?" Piglet asked.

Her father seemed disappointed, but nodded. He liked to meet Meena's friends and have a little conversation with them. But they usually preferred to hide themselves away upstairs.

Meena closed her bedroom door.

"Didn't you bring my bag?" she asked.

"No, I didn't," Pooh snapped. "It's still in the shed, with you-know-who."

Piglet had secretly hoped that Pooh might have got rid of the rabbit by now. "When are you going to let him out?"

"I'm not," said Pooh.

"Well, he can't stay there. What'll your mum and dad say if they find him?"

"I know he can't stay there. We've got to take him back."

"Back? Back where?"

"To school."

Piglet thought she must be dreaming this. "He's just escaped from there," she reminded Pooh.

"I know that, but he'll have to go back."

And then because Piglet looked unhappy and confused Pooh told her everything her dad had said.

"You see, we made a mistake. You can't let pets free like that. If he doesn't go back—he'll *die*." Pooh gave her words dramatic emphasis to impress on Piglet how serious this was.

"He'll die anyway when Mr Benson gets his hands on him," Piglet reminded her. A fact Pooh had managed to forget.

"Oh, no," she groaned. She sat down on Piglet's bed.

"What are we going to do?" asked Piglet.

For once Pooh was clean out of ideas. She shrugged her shoulders.

This made a pleasant change for Piglet. Pooh was usually so full of ideas that Piglet never managed to get one of hers in edgeways. Now was her chance.

"I'll tell you what I think," she said. Pooh looked up in surprise. Piglet ticked her ideas off on her fingers.

"One . . . we can't let Snuggles free because he wouldn't survive."

"I told you that,"
said Pooh.

"Two . . . we can't take Snuggles back to school. He wouldn't survive there for long either."

"I know that, as well."

"Three . . . we can't leave him in your shed."

"Tell me something I don't know," said Pooh irritably.

72

"So . . . four . . . we need to find someone else to take care of him. Some other animal lover."

"For instance?" said Pooh.

"RSPCA," said Piglet, in triumph.

Pooh thought about this. "But you know what happens there, don't you, if animals aren't claimed? It was on the news. They have to kill off loads of dogs every day cause no one wants them. There don't seem to be many animal lovers around."

Piglet sighed. "It's a *rabbit* lover we need."

Pooh began to smile. "Harold," she said. "Oh Piglet, you're brilliant."

Piglet glowed for a moment, then said, "Who's Harold?"

"St. John's Ambulance Harold," said Pooh, and she explained who he was to Piglet.

"Do you know where he lives?"

"Yeah, I've been there once or twice with my dad. We could take him round there now."

But first Piglet had to change out of her sari; it was supposed to be new for Diwali.

While she was changing Pooh said, in a matter of fact sort of way, "There's a reward, you know. Five pounds for whoever finds him. Nicola Wicks told my dad."

Piglet glanced at Pooh for a moment, then shrugged her shoulders. They didn't even need to talk about it. They both knew there were more important things than money.

"What will we do, though, when we get to this man's house?" asked Piglet.

Pooh could see her point. They could hardly knock on the door and say, "Please take care of this rabbit—we stole him from school."

"I don't know," said Pooh. "We can be thinking about that on the way."

As she struggled to keep up with Pooh, Piglet suggested, "Perhaps we could just leave him on the doorstep?"

"Like an abandoned baby," said Pooh, getting excited.

"With a note," added Piglet.

"'Please look after me', signed Snuggles, a rabbit in distress."

"We could disguise our writing," said Piglet.

They were a little disappointed they didn't have more time—they could have made one of those messages by cutting letters out of a magazine and then sticking them together, the kind blackmailers send.

"Great," said Pooh. She was feeling more lively, now they had a plan. "We'll write the note when we get to my house. Then we'll take Snuggles straight over."

"How?" said Piglet.

"What do you mean, how?" said Pooh, irritably.

"How will we get him there?"

"I don't know," said Pooh. "I can't think of everything."

"We could take him in a box," Piglet suggested.

"It would have to be *enormous*. Everyone would stare at us. And I bet he weighs a ton; we'd never carry him."

"We could push him in a wheelbarrow," said Piglet.

"Oh great. Why not dress him up in a frock and pretend it's for charity? We're trying to hide him, not advertise him."

"I meant—in a box—in a wheelbarrow," said Piglet.

They were definitely getting closer, but Pooh had a better idea still.

"A pram," she said. "That's what we need."

"Yeah," said Piglet. "Have you got one?"

"Not exactly," said Pooh. "But I know where I can get one. Come on, quick."

Chapter Eight

In which we find out what the baddies are up to and Pooh and Piglet take a rather large baby for a walk

Around six thirty, Nicola Wicks and Melanie Powell sat on a park bench. Nicola held a clipboard and a pen. She checked her watch.

"Oh, for goodness sake, where are they?"

Melanie looked around, willing them to come. "They'll be here in a minute."

"If they're not here in five minutes we'll start without them."

Nicola liked nothing better than making plans and bossing people, but with only Melanie to boss there didn't seem much point. The five minutes were almost up before Andrea and

Surendra drifted through the gates. Nicola was fizzing mad.

"Where have you been?" she demanded.

"The police station, of course," said Andrea.

"I don't see why it took so long."

"We had to give a statement and a description of Snuggles," said Andrea. "Then we had to sign it."

"I've never made a statement before," said Surendra.

Neither had Nicola. She began to sulk. She should have given herself the job of going to the police station. It would have been more exciting than asking shopkeepers to put up missing rabbit posters. Some of them were very rude to her. That dreadful Mr Curtis in the fish bar was the worst, making jokes about serving Snuggles up on the menu.

No wonder Philippa Curtis was so awful with a dad like that.

"Well, while you were sitting around in the police station," said Nicola nastily, "I was busy putting up posters. I thought we could stick these last two on lamp posts on the main road."

"That's against the law, fly-posting," said Andrea. "I read it in the police station."

Nicola looked at Andrea with contempt. "Personally *I* don't care, but of course if you're all too scared..."

The other girls looked away; no one was prepared to admit that.

"Right then, let's get on with it. We've searched the school field and we know Snuggles isn't there. But it's possible that when he starts to get hungry he'll head back to school, where he knows there's food. So we're going to set a trap for him."

"What sort of trap?" asked Melanie. She didn't like the sound of this. Melanie was definitely an animal lover.

"Only his hutch. We'll put it out on the school field with food and straw in it..."

"Ahhh, then it's all ready for him," said Melanie, picturing the exhausted rabbit crawling wearily into his own bed.

Andrea could soon see a problem with this. "Mr Benson will never let us into school at this time."

"We'll tell him Mrs Riley said he had to." Nicola was always prepared to tell the odd lie. "Anyway we'll need him to carry it out for us, it probably weighs a ton."

"He'll love that," said Andrea. "Him with his poor back."

"Come on," said Nicola. "Let's not waste any more time."

So the girls headed off down the main road. As they went along, Melanie wondered aloud, "What do you suppose Snuggles is doing right now? I wonder where he is?"

In case you're also wondering, the answers to those two questions are:

1. Reluctantly riding in a pram.
2. Less than a hundred metres away and coming straight towards them.

On the opposite side of the road, still in the distance, the netball girls suddenly spotted Pooh and Piglet, pushing a large carriage-built pram.

"Well, look who's coming," said Nicola.

"Ahh, they're walking the baby," said Andrea.

"I do love babies," said Surendra.

"Let's go and have a peep at the little darling," said Melanie.

What they couldn't have guessed was that 'the little darling' was in fact a very confused rabbit.

Getting Snuggles out of the shed and into the pram was the most difficult problem our heroines had faced so far. Borrowing the pram from Pooh's grandma was surprisingly easy.

It had been Pooh's pram when she was a baby and now it was being stored until her Auntie Marjorie needed it, some time before Christmas. Luckily Friday was her grandma's Bingo night and her grandad was in on his own. He hardly looked up from his gardening programme when Pooh told him she needed to borrow it.

Waking Snuggles up hadn't been a problem either. They'd just poked him gently with the garden hoe. But getting the rabbit into the pram had been an act of genius, in Pooh's opinion.

82

First they found a good strong box, baited it with bits of lettuce and carrot, then laid it on its side in the shed. After his nap Snuggles was a little peckish; he happily followed the bait into the box.

Before he could escape, the girls closed the flaps and turned the box onto its end. Then they struggled with it onto the edge of the pram and tipped the rabbit out.

So far so good.

But almost instantly Snuggles tried to escape. Pooh put up the pram hood and locked it, while Piglet threw the pram cover over the rabbit's head. They both struggled to hook it into place, trapping the large bump underneath.

In a flash Snuggles' face peeped out. But before he could blink Pooh had covered the whole pram with a cat net, in the hope that something intended to keep cats *out*, might also keep rabbits *in*.

It was only a light piece of muslin and would hardly have frustrated a butterfly. So the girls slipped handfuls of carrot and lettuce into the pram as an extra diversion. To their surprise this seemed to work. While Snuggles was quiet they set off for Harold's house, pushing the pram at speed down the main road.

"I'll be glad when we get there," said Piglet. "Everyone seems to be staring at us, as if they know what we've got in here."

Neither of the girls had realised how curious even complete strangers were about other people's babies. Every person they passed seemed to lean over, trying to get a peep.

"Just keep moving," said Pooh. "Whatever you do don't stop."

Soon they were nearly running, the pram bouncing up and down. This disturbed Snuggles again and a small black nose kept trying to poke its way round the edge of the cat net. Each time Pooh carefully covered it up, like a very fussy mother.

"We must try to be normal," she said.

"I don't *feel* normal," said Piglet. "I feel like a criminal." She imagined the word *kidnapper* might by now be printed on her forehead.

"Well, you're not," said Pooh. "Relax and everything will be fine."

"I just know someone is going to stop us and say, 'What have you two got in that pram?'"

"Nobody's going to do that," said Pooh.

But when she looked up she saw the dreaded netball team across the road, standing in a group, jeering at them.

"What have you two got in that pram?" shouted Nicola Wicks, above the sound of the passing cars.

"I told you so," whispered Piglet.

"For your information, it's my auntie's baby," Pooh shouted back.

"Baby what?" asked Andrea. All the girls burst out laughing.

"Baby elephant, if her family is anything to go by," said Nicola. At which point the netball girls started waving their arms around like trunks, pretending to be elephants.

"Come on, quick," said Piglet. "Before they cross the road."

But Pooh wasn't going to let them get away with that. The traffic was roaring past. She had to yell to make sure they heard her.

"My dad says if you come in our shop again he'll put *you* on the menu. 'Fried knickers and chips'." This was the nickname the braver boys at school sometimes called Nicola Wicks. Pooh couldn't have chosen a better insult. Nicola was furious.

Immediately she was frantically searching for a gap in the traffic to cross over and fulfil her promise to "do something" about Philippa Curtis. But wisely Pooh didn't wait around. She and Piglet raced as fast as they could in the opposite direction.

Fortunately for them the other girls persuaded Nicola to get on with the more important business of finding Snuggles. They could leave those two until next week at school, when they would plan a suitably nasty revenge for them.

Chapter Nine

In which our heroines' best-laid plan backfires and the caretaker receives a few visitors

"I *think* this is the one," said Pooh.

"Aren't you sure?" said Piglet.

"Well ... it's a long time since we came."

And certainly they did all look the same. The street was full of identical terraced houses with entries between, each leading to a pair of back gates. Pooh searched for some extra clue.

Snuggles was quiet now; the motion of the pram had finally lulled him to sleep. Piglet was afraid to stop in case he woke and tried to escape. So they kept on pushing the pram slowly up and down past Harold's house until Pooh was quite sure.

"Yes, that's the one, definitely. Come on."

"What if Harold looks out of the window and sees us open the gate?" asked Piglet anxiously.

"He might recognise *me*," said Pooh. "*You'd* better do it."

"On my own!" wailed Piglet.

"Okay. Don't panic," said Pooh. "I know, one of us can run down the entry and knock really hard on the back gate. Then when Harold goes to see who it is we'll quickly open his front gate, put Snuggles on the step, ring the doorbell and run off. He'll come back into the house, open the front door and find Snuggles there waiting for him."

"What about us?"

"By then we'll be at the other end of the road, no problem."

Piglet felt sure there was a serious flaw in Pooh's plan but she couldn't for the life of her see what it was, so she nodded.

"I'll look after the pram," she said. "You can go down the entry."

Pooh sighed, she might have guessed. She sneaked along the entry and hammered loudly on Harold's gate. Then she dashed back up the entry, expecting Piglet to be at the front gate waiting for her. But the loud banging had scared Piglet so much she was disappearing

down the road with the pram. Pooh followed her, grabbed the pram and Piglet and rushed them both back to Harold's house.

It was only as the gate closed behind them that the serious flaw in Pooh's plan occurred to them. Without the cardboard box, which they'd left at home in the shed, how were they going to get Snuggles out of the pram?

There was really no alternative.

"Come on," said Pooh. "We'll have to lift him out."

"With our hands?" said Piglet.

"Yes," said Pooh. "With our hands. Quick."

She tore off the cat net and peeled back the pram cover, quite prepared to face the terrible task. But with one bound Snuggles leapt out unaided and immediately tried to climb over the low wall around Harold's front garden. The girls pulled him back, grabbing any bits of fur they could get hold of. In their desperation all fear of the rabbit disappeared.

Having prevented his escape their next problem was to keep hold of him. He kept giving them the slip. He raced round the small garden with surprising speed. Every time they managed to corner him he shot past them or between their legs.

"Quick, behind you," squealed Piglet.

"Don't stand there," hissed Pooh. "Stop him. Head him off with the pram."

The girls ran around in circles, Snuggles leading them, so that it was a few moments before they realised they were no longer alone. Their shouts had drawn Harold down his entry and now he leaned against the corner of the house with a smile on his face.

"Who's winning?" he asked.

The girls stopped racing; even Snuggles stopped and turned.

"Are you two looking for me?"

The girls just looked at one another without speaking.

"It's Philippa, isn't it?" he asked.

Pooh nodded; she could hardly deny it.

Harold leaned over his wall and grabbed Snuggles by the soft fold of skin at the back of his neck. He held the rabbit tenderly but firmly, and asked, "Does this magnificent creature belong to you?"

"No," said Pooh. Then, "That is . . . sort of . . . no," she finally decided.

Harold turned to Piglet.

"No," she gasped. She didn't want responsibility for him.

"Well, he must belong to someone. He's obviously escaped. I'll go and ring the police."

"Oh, don't do that," begged Pooh.

And Piglet, almost in tears, added, "Please, Harold."

"I think you two had better tell me exactly what's going on," said Harold.

Pooh and Piglet nodded. Now they were in big trouble.

Meanwhile, back at school, Mrs Riley's car pulled into the school car park. She'd come straight from the dentist where she'd had three fillings. Although the feeling was at last beginning to return, the right side of her face still felt swollen and lopsided.

But despite the discomfort, Mrs Riley had been unable to stop thinking about the missing rabbit. She knew she wouldn't rest happily until she had cleared up this dreadful business. So, hoping it wasn't too late, she had returned to school to tackle the caretaker.

She knew Mr Benson didn't like to be disturbed at the weekend, but this was a serious matter. She knocked on the door of the caretaker's bungalow. His wife answered, wiping her hands on her apron.

Mrs Benson, unlike her husband, was a warm and friendly person. Living, as they did, inside the school grounds, they had no close neighbours and didn't see many people from day to day. Mrs Benson regretted this. She loved to bake and always had tins full of cakes and scones, just in case anyone should visit.

"Mrs Riley. Do come in," she said. "I'll put the kettle on. I'm sure you'll have a cup of tea."

"I came to see Mr Benson, really." The headteacher was determined to be firm with the caretaker; it might be difficult if this turned into a social visit, with tea and scones.

"Well, come on in. I'm afraid you'll find him on his back. Flat out," she smiled.

94

She led Mrs Riley into the living room where the caretaker lay, as she had said, flat out on the carpet with his eyes closed. (He was pretending to be asleep.)

"Oh, dear," said Mrs Riley. "He does look bad. Is he ill?" In fact he looked exactly like a dead body.

"His back's gone," his wife whispered.

"He must be in a lot of pain," Mrs Riley whispered back.

"Terrible," whispered Mrs Benson cheerfully.

"I am here, you know," the caretaker interrupted them. "I can speak for myself. It's my back that's gone, not my voice."

Mrs Benson smiled, ignoring his bad temper. "I'm sure you'd like some tea, Mrs Riley. And a rock bun. They're freshly made."

Mrs Riley shuddered. "Oh, no, thank you. I've come straight from the dentist. I won't have anything to eat, but a cup of tea would be very welcome, if it's no trouble."

Mrs Benson went into the kitchen leaving them together.

Mrs Riley took a deep breath and began, "Mr Benson, there's something I want to say to you..."

"I'll bet there is," thought the caretaker, expecting a full admission of guilt. But Mrs Riley, standing directly over him, made *him* feel at a disadvantage. He didn't like that at all.

"Won't you sit down first?" he said.

"No, thank you." Mrs Riley felt more in control in this position; she remained standing. "I must say, Mr Benson, I am very sorry..."

"Oh, you don't have to apologise," he interrupted, slightly rising up. "It's not the way I'd have got rid of the rabbit. But if that's the way you wanted to do it, it's okay by me. The main thing is it's gone. Now we're all happy. Or I will be as soon as I get back on my feet."

Mrs Riley was completely confused. "Apologise?" she said. "I think it's you that should be apologising..."

"Me!" replied the caretaker, his voice rising to a shout. He couldn't imagine what she meant. He struggled to lift himself up from the carpet. "Apologise! Me?"

For a minute they glared at one another, without a word.

Just then Mrs Benson came through from the kitchen carrying a tray, quite unaware of the tension in the room.

"Isn't it nice, dear, having a visitor? We rarely have an excuse to get out the best china. This is such a lovely surprise."

Mrs Riley smiled awkwardly. Mr Benson groaned and sank back onto the carpet. At that moment there was an insistent ringing on the front door bell.

"Now I wonder who that can be." Mrs Benson's face lit up at the prospect of more visitors and further cups of tea.

She opened the door, still smiling. Nicola and the other three girls stood outside smiling back. Their uniform politeness concealed their determination to get their own way.

"I'm sorry to bother you," said Nicola, in a sickly, sweet voice. "I wonder if we could see Mr Benson?"

"Yes, of course, dear. Come on in," said his wife kindly. She added, "He's not too well, I'm afraid," but her words were drowned out by the caretaker's angry shout from the living room.

"No, they can't see me. Tell them to clear off. Don't they know it's Friday night? Haven't they got anything else to do, Brownies to go to?"

Mrs Benson gave the girls an embarrassed smile. "Don't you mind Mr Benson, his back's hurting him. These girls are too big for Brownies," she called back to him. "Why don't you come tomorrow?" she whispered.

"But we need to get into school *now*," said Nicola. "It's a matter of life and death."

"Tell them to go away," Mr Benson called again. "Coming here, bothering me. They'll be sorry on Monday."

Nicola leaned inside the doorway, causing Mrs Benson to step back. She spoke up, to ensure the caretaker heard her. "Mr Benson will be *sorry* if he doesn't give us that key. I should tell you that we have the full support of Mrs Riley. She'll be very angry when she hears that Mr Benson has hindered our investigations."

Mrs Riley had kept out of the whole thing while it seemed to have nothing to do with her. On hearing her own name she felt compelled to go to the door.

"...We're going to have to report this to her on Monday. Then we'll see who's sorry..."

Nicola continued, but her words trailed away as the headteacher's face appeared beside Mrs Benson's at the front door. Nicola swallowed hard.

"What exactly is it that I'm fully in support of?" asked Mrs Riley.

Nicola stepped back and attempted to hide herself behind the other girls who wore matching expressions of bright pink. Mrs Benson, embarrassed on their behalf and always anxious to ease a difficult situation, said, "Why don't you girls come in and I'll make you some orange. Perhaps you could eat a rock bun. Come along. Don't be shy." And she ushered them in.

"Don't bring them in here," said the caretaker. "Send them home."

But by now the four girls, plus the headteacher, were crowded into the caretaker's small living room, arranged around him in a circle. They looked down on him as he lay on the rug, trying to hold on to a little bit of dignity.

"Don't stand round like a set of skittles," he grumbled. "If you're coming in at least sit down."

The girls reluctantly sat down and studied their feet.

"Now, what is this business about?" asked Mrs Riley. The girls remained silent. "Nicola?"

"Well," said Nicola, for once completely lost for words. "I thought...that is we all thought...actually I think it was Melanie's idea..."

There was a sharp intake of breath from Melanie. "No it was not."

"I seem to remember it was *your* idea, *actually*," Andrea reminded her.

Nicola ground her teeth and sighed heavily.

"Go on," Mrs Riley encouraged her. "Tell us what this wonderful idea was."

Nicola struggled to put an excuse together but she was saved by the doorbell which suddenly rang again.

"Gordon Bennett," moaned the caretaker. "It's worse than Piccadilly Circus. Doesn't anyone know it's Friday night?"

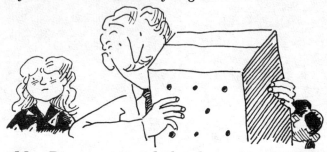

Mrs Benson opened the door. A man she'd never seen before stood smiling at her. He was carrying a large cardboard box with holes in it. Hanging back unhappily, as if they would have liked to crawl under a pair of matching stones, were Pooh and Piglet.

"Do you mind if we come in and speak to the caretaker?" asked Harold.

"Oh no, why not," they clearly heard the caretaker reply. "Join the party, why don't you. Don't mind me. I only live here."

Mrs Benson smiled apologetically. She showed them through.

"I'll put the kettle on," she whispered.

a nice cup of tea

Harold walked in and Pooh and Piglet followed him. They tried to find a bit of space that wasn't occupied by the caretaker or other people's feet.

They stood either side of Mr Benson's shoulders like a pair of bookends.

Harold looked around at the assembled group. They looked expectantly back at him and the large cardboard box. He directed his question generally into the room.

"Has anybody lost a rabbit, by any chance?"

The caretaker groaned, as though he were in real pain, and closed his eyes.

Chapter Ten

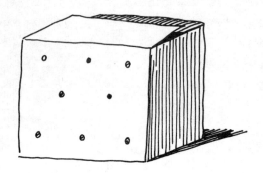

In which all is resolved—happily for some, not so happily for others

Everyone sat up with great interest—everyone except Mr Benson; he sank lower, if that was possible.

"Oh no," he thought, "I should have done it in while I had the chance."

Of course, he's assuming that it's Snuggles inside Harold's box. But he's wrong. Mr Benson is in for an even bigger surprise.

"Can I get you a cup of tea?" asked Mrs Benson, popping in again.

"That would be lovely," said Harold.

"What about you two girls? I suppose you all know each other?"

Pooh and Piglet nodded across the room at the netball team and the netball team glared back. You could have cut the air with a cake slice. Mrs Benson went out to get more drinks.

"Do you mind sitting down, if you're staying," said the caretaker. "I do hate being looked down on."

The netball girls squeezed up together on the settee.

Pooh and Piglet shared one armchair.

Mrs Riley occupied the other.

Harold sat on the edge of a dining chair, the cardboard box perched on his knee.

"I'm the headteacher of the school," said Mrs Riley. "Are you telling us you have our rabbit in that box?"

"Well...not exactly," said Harold, "but I know where he is."

The netball team looked furious. Someone had beaten them to the reward.

Mr Benson looked pretty mad too. He just wanted everybody to go home.

Pooh and Piglet looked like two convicted criminals awaiting sentence.

Mrs Riley looked relieved. Snuggles was still alive. She'd apparently misjudged the caretaker.

"So if it isn't Snuggles in the box, what have you got in there?" she enquired.

"Before I tell you that, I should tell you something interesting about that rabbit of yours." Pooh and Piglet shuddered. Now it was surely going to come out.

"Anyone for more tea?" Mrs Benson again interrupted.

more tea ?

"No, no," said the caretaker. "No more cups of tea. Let him get on with it."

He could see this turning into a complete pantomime; his house filling up with unwelcome visitors, standing around looking down on him, drinking *his* tea and eating *his* food.

"I'm sorry. Don't mind me. You carry on with your story," she apologised. "This is so nice. I can't remember when we last had such a houseful."

Harold smiled. "I don't know if you realise it but Snuggles is quite a rare animal."

Mr Benson grunted. "He certainly had a rare pair of teeth."

"How do you mean 'rare'?" asked Mrs Riley.

"He's a Blanc de Bouscat. That's French, you know," said Harold proudly.

"It sounds more like a bottle of wine," muttered Mr Benson.

"He's worth a lot of money to a breeder like me," Harold continued.

The headteacher smiled. "Really!" she said.

"I understand that lately he's been a bit of a problem," said Harold. "Grown too big for his hutch, not very friendly, biting people, I hear."

The caretaker frowned; Mrs Riley shifted uncomfortably in her chair.

"If you want my opinion, Snuggles isn't what you'd call ideal pet material," said Harold.

"You can say that again," said Mr Benson.

"Actually," said Mrs Riley, "we have been considering the possibility of finding him a new home. It would have to be somewhere we knew he would be happy, of course."

"Naturally," said Harold.

"Do *you* have any ideas?" asked Mrs Riley.

"Well, as a matter of fact, *I'd* be pleased to take Snuggles off your hands."

Mrs Riley beamed. This was all most satisfactory. Even Mr Benson smiled, thinking he'd got rid of the rabbit, until Harold continued, "And in return I'd provide you with more suitable animals, smaller, more attractive to children. And I'd always be on hand should there be any problems. In short we could have an arrangement whereby I'd provide you with a regular supply of baby rabbits."

"Rabbits!" hissed the caretaker, emphasising the plural.

"How many were you thinking of?" asked Mrs Riley, also a little uncertain.

"One for each class?" suggested Harold.

"That's ten," Nicola chimed in.

"And one for the nursery," said Andrea.

"Eleven then," said Harold. "I can take one home." And he opened the box he was holding and out popped a dozen baby rabbits.

Like a chorus coming in perfectly on cue there was a ripple of "Ohhh" and "Ahhh..."

The effect was only marred by a heartfelt moan from Mr Benson. "Christopher Columbus."

Everyone wanted to hold one of the rabbits.

"It's going to be very difficult to choose one to send back," said Mrs Riley.

"It doesn't seem fair," said Andrea.

"Can't we keep them all?" said Melanie.

"Why not," agreed the head.

"I could quite fancy one," said Mrs Benson.

"There's plenty more where these came

from," said Harold. "I've got a breeding pair *you* could have."

"Over my dead body," said Mr Benson.

Pooh and Piglet were so thrilled at the appearance of the rabbits they almost forgot they were still under threat. But as soon as they began to relax Mrs Riley said, "Where exactly did you find Snuggles, Mr . . . erm?"

"Barber. Harold Barber. He just turned up in my front garden. Can you believe it? Fortunately Philippa and Meena here were able to tell me where he came from. It was lucky they did or I'd probably never have found out."

"Well done, you two," said Mrs Riley.

The netball team glared harder. Pooh and Piglet sat quietly, afraid to believe their luck.

"So all's well that ends well," said Harold.

"Oh, I do agree," said Mrs Riley. "But then as I've always said: every problem has its own elegant solution."

"What about the reward?" Nicola asked. In her opinion it wasn't *such* an elegant solution.

Mrs Riley had forgotten the reward. "Oh

yes," she sighed. "I suppose we should offer it to Mr Barber. He found the rabbit."

"Oh, I'm not interested in a reward," said Harold. "I've got Snuggles. Perhaps Philippa and Meena could share it. They helped me round him up. They've been most helpful girls."

Pooh and Piglet couldn't believe their ears. What a nice man Harold was, they thought.

"Very well, see me at school you two. I'll present it in Assembly on Monday morning. It'll be an excellent opportunity to tell the rest of the school about our new additions."

The two girls beamed at one another. It wasn't so much the money they were interested in as the glory—having it announced in Assembly.

Even more than this, it was knowing that they had seen a wrong that needed putting right—and they'd put it right. That was their reward. However, they weren't about to turn down five pounds. There was a lot you could buy with five pounds. Pooh squeezed Piglet's arm. Piglet smiled back.

Determined to tie up the loose ends, Mrs Riley turned to the netball girls. "I think you girls had also better come to see me on Monday morning. By then I hope you'll have an explanation for your very strange behaviour."

110

The netball team sulked on the settee. Seeing this Mrs Benson offered another round of drinks and biscuits to cheer them up. Nicola Wicks took two and slipped one in her pocket, thinking no one had seen her. But everybody had.

Hoping it might make everyone disappear, Mr Benson closed his eyes and reflected on how things had turned out. He'd got rid of one wretched rabbit only to get lumbered with twelve more. He thought of the mess, he thought of the extra work and he thought of the dozen new hutches cluttering up the school. And he thought of all the future baby rabbits they might produce. It was like a nightmare.

And, inevitably, he thought of Snuggles. He could just imagine the pleasure it would give that animal, if it knew the damage it had caused. Mr Benson could almost believe it might have been planned—The Rabbit's Final Revenge.

But there was nothing he could do about it. He gave a last defeated sigh and fell asleep. In minutes the caretaker was snoring loudly. Everyone politely pretended not to notice, but they dropped their voices, so they wouldn't disturb him.

And finally you must be wondering—what of the poor victim of this story? Does he have a happy ending? Well, of course.

Safe and sound now in the back garden of Harold's house, Snuggles sat contentedly looking around him. In rows of hutches, stacked three deep along the walls of the garden, dozens of other rabbits gazed down on the prize new addition to Harold's rabbit collection. Snuggles wallowed in the admiration of the other rabbits. He could tell he was going to like it here. He had plenty of room, lots to eat and, at last, the kind of appreciation he felt he had always deserved.